Badru Rising

BOOK 3

BY: Davy DeGreeff

visit us at www.abdopublishing.com

To to my parents. I'm forever in debt to your love and support, and I hope I've made you proud—DD

Published by Magic Wagon, a division of the ABDO Group, 8000 West 78th Street, Edina, Minnesota 55439. Copyright © 2010 by Abdo Consulting Group, Inc. International copyrights reserved in all countries. All rights reserved. No part of this book may be reproduced in any form without written permission from the publisher.

Calico Chapter Books™ is a trademark and logo of Magic Wagon.

Printed in the United States.

Text by Davy DeGreeff
Cover and chapter Illustrations by Sam Brookins
Edited by Stephanie Hedlund and Rochelle Baltzer
Cover and interior design by Jaime Martens

Library of Congress Cataloging-in-Publication Data

DeGreeff, Davy, 1984-
  Tommy Bomani : Badru rising / by Davy DeGreeff ; illustrated by Sam Brookins.
      p. cm. -- (Tommy Bomani, teen warrior ; bk. 3)
  Summary: Although an ancient prophecy foretells his death, twelve-year-old Tommy Bomani, who inherited his powerful strength and shape-shifting ability from an Egyptian god, prepares to battle the evil wizard Badru, with help from the Protectorate, a small group of adults in Tommy's community.
  ISBN 978-1-60270-699-6
  [1. Supernatural--Fiction. 2. Prophecies--Fiction. 3. Magic--Fiction. 4. Egyptian Americans--Fiction. 5. Youths' writings. 6. Youths' art.]
  I. Brookins, Sam, 1984- ill. II. Title. III. Title: Badru rising.
  PZ7.D36385Tm 2009
  [Fic]--dc22
                                        2009009458

Contents

Trial Run

A man's dark shadow slithered across the dusty Egyptian street. He stood among the rushing traffic of hurried bodies and smiled. The crowd kept its distance on either side of him, closing him in a bubble of empty space.

No one would walk near the man. They were all afraid of him, and not one of them knew why. Their eyes stayed frozen to the ground, terrified of accidentally catching his gaze.

The Egyptians had never seen this man before, but they seemed to know him. He was like a familiar character from a frightening childhood tale of danger, demons, and darkness.

The man toyed with their fear, leaning toward an old woman and staring at a young man. He wanted to see them quicken their pace past him. It pleased him that thousands of years past his prime, he could still frighten people without a word.

The man spotted a young boy, sitting alone and playing with a rag doll. He moved toward the boy slowly and silently.

The boy twirled his doll like a gymnast, bending it this way and that. He noticed a dark shadow had replaced the afternoon sun and looked up. Then, he began to scream.

The boy's mother recognized her son's cry and dropped the fish she'd been holding. She shoved through the crowd, horrified to find what could make her boy so scared. When she saw what had caused his fear, she began to scream as well.

The man looked deep into the woman's eyes. She froze on the spot, unable to break his gaze. The man smiled a slow, wicked smile. Then without a word, he disappeared on the sandy Egyptian breeze.

The woman snapped out of her spell. She ran to her crying child and held him tightly, trying unsuccessfully to hide her own fear.

The man appeared again dozens of miles away in a worn cave on the edge of the desert. He stood at the cave entrance and stared at the setting sun. After years in exile, he felt his purpose reborn.

At last he was ready. Badru was ready to cast his presence on the world once more.

The Protectorate

CHAPTER 1

Tommy lifted his eyebrows and looked questioningly at the police detective before him. The detective rubbed the day-old beard growing on his chin. He looked at Tommy through permanently squinted eyes and chuckled.

"I guess Asim wasn't kidding," Detective Matthews said. "Talking to you is like stepping into a time machine and yakking with your dad fifteen years ago. You go right for the throat."

Tommy didn't budge. "I was told that all of my questions would be answered."

The detective looked to Asim, who nodded. Matthews shrugged. "So be it, I guess."

When he had returned from Florida a little over a month ago, Tommy and Asim had had a very long talk. Eventually, Asim had turned over every secret detail of the Bomani family tale.

With a deep breath, Asim had started at the beginning of the amazing story. He told Tommy how the goddess Bastet had fallen in love with a

6

human slave. The couple named their first and only child Bomani.

Bastet's father, the sun king Ra, was ashamed and demanded that she destroy the child. Instead, she ran away and hid among regular people. She disguised her true nature as she raised her son. When the time came, Bastet watched Bomani battle the evil Badru and become the finest warrior Egypt had ever known.

It had taken Asim hours to tell the story. When he finished, Tommy had made him tell it a second time. With every word, Tommy had felt more and more proud to wear a fragment of Ra's statue around his neck.

At the same time, Tommy began to realize that he wasn't just fighting for himself or for his friends. He was fighting for the hundreds of Bomani warriors, men and women, who had come before him and bravely battled Badru. Despite his pride, Tommy felt a little overwhelmed.

Next, Asim told Tommy about a great web of supporters scattered across the globe. They were called the Protectorate. Asim swore they were as committed to the fight against Badru as any

Bomani had ever been. They honorably served in a number of different roles, from gathering information to physically fighting in battle. Detective Matthews was a member of that group.

Matthews looked exactly opposite how Tommy imagined a detective would look. He was short, wide, hairy, middle-aged, and smelled a little like cheese. Still, Tommy had no trouble believing he was as important a friend as Asim claimed. Despite his appearance, Matthews's eyes sparkled with intelligence, and he looked strong enough to punch through a brick wall.

Asim had brought the detective here to answer Tommy's questions about the Protectorate. Tommy had always thought only a handful of people knew about his ancient mission and Ra's golden statue. This new information brought to mind a few questions that he was interested in having answered.

But so far, the answers were slow in coming. Tommy began to tap his foot.

"Where were you when I needed the police to stop Fisk the first time?" Tommy asked for the second time in two minutes.

The detective smiled and answered, "I've been in Europe for a year training with international police. Top secret kinda stuff. I just got back a couple weeks ago." His voice was gravelly, but warm.

"How much do you know about me? And about what I have to do?"

"I know plenty about what you have to do. I was a friend of your father's in my much, much younger days. I'm afraid I don't know much about you, though. Yet. Asim says you're figuring things out quickly. That's good." He looked to Asim, who gave a single nod.

Tommy decided to test his limits. Next he asked, "What do you think about the prophecy?"

Detective Matthews's eyebrows raised slightly. He looked to Asim, who nodded once more and said, "Tommy and I have a partnership of complete honesty, Detective. Speak freely."

The detective shrugged, then said, "I think it's a bunch of garbage, to be frank."

"Really?" Tommy said, surprised.

The prophecy had been a source of interest for Tommy ever since Asim had finally told him the legend of Badru. Asim told Tommy that Badru had suffered in the desert for days after his fight with the pharaoh's guards. There, he had dreamed of a great deciding battle between himself and an extraordinarily powerful supernatural child.

In the dream, Badru had won. Or so he claimed.

The prophecy had leaked through time like a fairy tale. It was told at campfires and bedtimes. It was taken differently in different circles. For the followers of Badru, it was a prediction of his victory. For supernatural families, it was a warning to keep powerful children from chasing battles too large for them to understand.

Then, Tommy was born with both Wolfe and Bomani blood flowing through him. This made people wonder if the prophecy was possible.

"How can you say that?" Tommy asked.

"Because it seems like rubbish," Detective Matthews answered. "First, it happened a couple thousand years before you were born. Second, there isn't anything exactly impressive about Badru predicting that *some kid* at *some point* would challenge him to a great battle."

Tommy stopped him. "But he specifically mentioned my mom. He said that a Bomani would have a child with a member of a powerful tribe—"

"Who doesn't develop the power she inherits? Is that what you were going to say?" Matthews shook his head. "That is just one of *dozens* of versions I've heard. I'm sure Asim has told you versions that differed from the one you first heard."

Tommy nodded reluctantly.

"No one knows what Badru really dreamed, or if he even dreamed anything. People retelling the story over hundreds of years have altered his words. This is how fairy tales work, and why they always seem almost possible. For all we know, what people think he dreamed isn't anything close to what he actually did. But because people believe it, they give it power and think it's true."

"But what if that is what he dreamed? And what if he's right?"

Matthews shrugged. "Then I guess you're going to die."

CHAPTER 2

A Gut Feeling

T ommy looked the detective in the eye and said, "But you don't think he's right?"

"No," Matthews answered. "His followers believe in the prophecy because they think it means they are destined to win. But I knew your father, and I know there is no way his son would ever allow Badru to succeed."

Tommy thought about this. Asim had given him the same interpretation, and so had Burt. But the idea still bothered him. How could he not be bothered by a prediction about his death that was made before he was even born?

"The bottom line, Tommy, is that Badru predicted you would be born. This has come true. He predicted that you would be special. This is also true. The next step is up to you. He predicted a great, final battle that he would win. I think he's wrong."

Tommy blushed. He was still having trouble believing that one of his ancestors had been an

Egyptian god. On top of that, the people who knew respected that little bit of mystical blood that coursed through him. It was difficult to accept that he was as special as people told him.

"But how can you think I'll win?" Tommy asked. "Until half an hour ago, you'd never even met me."

"Call it a gut feeling. Call it a hunch. I call it faith that good will triumph over evil because that's the way it's supposed to be."

Asim put his hand on Matthews's shoulder and said, "Is that enough of an answer for you, Tommy?"

"Yes. Thank you."

"You're welcome," Matthews answered. Then his tone became more businesslike. "Now if you don't mind, I was hoping you could help me find some answers."

"About Fisk?"

"Exactly."

Tommy sighed and took a seat on the warehouse floor. "I just don't know how much help I'll be."

"Is there anything you can remember that might help? The direction he went in? Any hint at where Badru is hiding?"

"Nothing. He went back out of the forest the way he'd come in. All he said was that they had a 'long journey' back to Badru."

Tommy thought about that rainy Florida night and shuddered. Within ten minutes he had lost a piece of Ra's statue and nearly lost his best friend.

Detective Matthews grunted. "We may not know where he is, but that doesn't mean we won't find him. I have connections around the world, and they are all looking for Fisk. It's only a matter of time."

Tommy paused. He wanted to ask a question, but he was almost afraid of the answer. "Do you think he would come back here?"

"With someone that crazy, nothing is impossible. But I'd be surprised if he did. He knows you'll be well protected. There are too many eyes searching for him."

Tommy bit his lip and nodded. He stood to shake the detective's hand.

"Thank you, Detective Matthews. I feel better knowing I have people like you on my side."

"There are more of us than you can imagine. We're counting on you, but we're also here to help in any way we can. Make sure to let me know if you see anything that doesn't feel right, okay? Anything at all that jumps out at you. Don't be afraid to call me."

"No problem."

"Thank you for coming, old friend," Asim said, shaking Matthews's hand. "With you back at our side, Badru's days are surely numbered."

CHAPTER 3

Guests

Tommy and Asim walked the detective across the sprawling warehouse to the front door. Tommy pulled the door open and sunlight pierced the dusty, dim interior. Detective Matthews nodded at Tommy and walked to his car.

Asim waited until he was out of earshot, then asked Tommy, "What do you think?"

"Of Detective Matthews?"

"Yes. And of what he said."

"He seems nice. And he didn't candy-coat things. I like that," Tommy answered.

"He respects you," Asim said. "You should be honored. Detective Matthews is one of the finest men I've ever known. He often understands people better than they understand themselves."

"Do you think he can help us?"

"I'd be pressed to think of anyone more able, or willing, to try."

Just then, a familiar gigantic shadow covered them from the open door.

"Burt, you're late. That's unusual for you," Asim said calmly.

Burt pointed behind him. "I know, and I apologize. But I was escorting a guest."

A round man in his forties with a glowing smile stepped around Burt and through the door. He glanced everywhere, trying to take in everything at once.

"So this is where the real action happens."

"Mr. Walker," Asim greeted the guest with a smile. "I'm so glad you could finally see how much good your generosity has done." The two men shook hands.

"Oh, I'd hardly say finding you an abandoned warehouse is 'generosity.' But I'm more than willing to accept your flattery." Mr. Walker winked at Tommy and continued to stare at his surroundings. He looked as if he were at the Grand Canyon, and not in a dusty warehouse full of boxes, tarps, and shadows.

Mr. Walker was the father of Tommy's classmate, Lily. He was also the curator for the history museum and a member of the Protectorate. He had called in a favor so Tommy could train in this building.

Asim looked at the doorway. "And Annie is here as well. How are you, dear?"

Tommy's cousin walked inside with her gaze cast over her shoulder. She turned to face Asim, with a puzzled look. "Could be worse, I guess."

Mr. Walker began talking excitedly. "Asim, is there somewhere we could speak?"

"Of course. We have an office in the back." Asim turned to Burt. "Would you begin the readying, please?"

"Yes, sir," Burt said. He watched Asim and Mr. Walker walk away. Then he let the door slip shut and looked at Tommy. "Tommy, I don't mean to panic you, but it's shape-shifting time. We've got something a bit more important than training to worry about at the moment."

"What are you talking about?" Tommy asked.

Annie spoke up. "We're pretty sure someone followed Mr. Walker here."

"After Mr. Walker drove by us," Burt said, "we looked back up the hill where he had come from and saw a guy on a bike. When he saw us looking, he bolted into the trees."

"Did it look like one of Fisk's men?" said Tommy.

"We couldn't tell. He was too far away," Annie

said. "But when we were walking in, I think I saw someone in the bushes."

"Tommy, what if someone's figured out what's going on here?" Burt whispered fiercely, afraid someone was listening from the shadows.

"Asim says that we're only able to look for the remaining statue pieces because regular people don't know about them," Tommy muttered. "If someone followed Mr. Walker and knows more than we would like them to . . ."

"Exactly," Burt said. "We need to figure out what's going on and fast. Any ideas?"

Annie cleared her throat. "Well, it's not the most complicated plan in the world, but . . . do either of you have a tennis ball handy?"

The warehouse door flew open with a crash and Burt and Tommy ran out. Tommy held an old tennis ball and waved it toward the open door.

"Come on, Biscuit!" he yelled. "Here, girl!"

Annie ran out from the dark doorway, fully transformed into a large, shaggy dog. She stared at the ball as if it was the juiciest steak she'd ever seen. She barked and jumped in anticipation.

"Ready, Biscuit?" Tommy asked, and then threw the ball next to Mr. Walker's car. "Fetch!"

Annie bolted and snapped the ball up in her teeth. She ran back to Burt, dropped the ball at his feet, and then spun back to face the car.

"This is gonna be a long one, girl. Here we go!" Burt said. Then he hurled the ball into the trees.

Annie dashed after it like a bolt of lightning. The boys waited. After half a minute of silence, Burt looked to Tommy, who shrugged.

Tommy held his breath until he couldn't take it anymore. But as soon as he took his first step forward, Annie came back out. She was growling and using her teeth to drag a surprised young girl by the sleeve of her sweatshirt.

"Lily?" Burt and Tommy said at the same time.

"Get this dog off of me!" Lily Walker screamed.

Tommy hesitated, confused. Then, he snapped to his senses enough to call out. "Annie—I mean, Biscuit! Let her go!"

Annie did as she was told and trotted back to the boys, pleased her plan had worked.

"Lily, what are you doing here?" Tommy asked.

Lily stood up and dusted the dirt off of her jeans. "Oh, come on Tommy. You know what I was doing. I followed my dad here."

"But why?"

She stopped and looked at him like he was missing something. "Do you really think my father could keep something like this hidden from me?"

Burt shot a panicked look to Tommy. "We, um, we don't know what you're talking about."

"That Asim guy and my dad always sneak off at weird hours," Lily explained. "I knew something was up, so I followed them. Sorry to spy or whatever, but I was curious."

Burt was sweating bullets and looked sick to his stomach. "Really, really don't know what you mean. I don't know of anything weird, and . . ."

Lily looked up to the sky and stomped her foot in frustration. "Well, how about this? Seeing as she just put teeth marks all over this one, your stupid cousin owes me a new sweatshirt."

Tommy froze. "Maybe we should go inside and talk about this," he said.

Burt led the slow march back to the door. "I'll get Asim. I can't wait to hear what he thinks of this."

CHAPTER 4

Full House

T he next morning, the smell of sizzling breakfast drew Tommy into the kitchen. He grabbed a plate from the cupboard and accepted a peck on the cheek from his mother. Then, he took a heaping helping of bacon, eggs, and potatoes. He set his plate on the table and dug in without saying good morning to his aunt or cousin.

"Slow down there, Lil' Warrior," Mrs. Bomani said. "Choking on your breakfast is no way to start the day."

"Oh, he's almost a teenager. If you want him to start growing, and I know you do, you'll let him eat all he wants," smirked Tommy's aunt Kirsten.

Kirsten and Annie had moved into the Bomani house about a month ago. Their family reunion in Florida had reminded both sisters how much they had missed each other. They decided to make up for lost time, and the best way to do that was to be as close as possible. So Kirsten sold their house and got a job at Tommy's mom's law office. Annie started attending Tommy's school. So far things had worked out pretty well.

"You were yelling in your sleep again, doofus," Annie said.

"Sorry," Tommy muttered.

At the moment, the biggest issue was the sleeping arrangements. Mrs. Bomani and Aunt Kirsten both needed their own rooms. There was only one room in the house to spare: Tommy's. Luckily it had been decided that Tommy could keep his private space. But, that meant Annie was camped out on the sofa bed in the downstairs living room next to Tommy's room.

"Are you having more of those dreams, Tommy?" his mom asked. "Do you want to talk about them?" she offered.

"Naw. Thanks, though." Tommy shrugged.

"So, Tommy," Annie started. "What are we going to do about the Walker girl?"

"We aren't going to do anything," Tommy answered. "Asim said Mr. Walker talked with Lily, and she's not going to tell anyone."

Mrs. Bomani interjected. "I'm just glad it was only Lily Walker who found out. Imagine who else could be eavesdropping."

"Oh, I'm sure Asim wasn't happy either way," Kirsten said.

"He wasn't. But he and Burt figured we'll just have to be thankful this time it wasn't one of Badru's spies listening in. We're going to be way more careful in the future," Tommy said.

Mrs. Bomani smiled and topped off Tommy's orange juice. "Burt's really taking to Asim's teaching, isn't he?"

Tommy nodded. Burt was also improving in battle strategy. Occasionally, he even found solutions to problems that had stumped Asim. He was almost like a whole new kid.

"Tommy, we gotta go!" Annie said, jumping up. "My history test! I have to slam through the chapter first or Mr. Charles is gonna eat me alive!"

Tommy shoveled a pile of potatoes into his mouth and chased them with a gulp of juice.

"I'm coming," he said. He grabbed his backpack from the floor and met his cousin at the door.

"Have a good day, kids!" said Mrs. Bomani.

Aunt Kirsten called after them, "And you'd better do well on that test, young lady! Or you'll have more that just Mr. Charles to answer to!"

CHAPTER 5

Old Friends

"I'll be right back," Tommy said to Burt and Annie. He dumped the rest of his chicken nuggets into the waste bin. Then, he put his tray on the counter and headed to Lily's table. Lily sat with the most popular kids in Tommy's grade. Most of them weren't usually friendly, so he wasn't sure how this was going to go over.

Tommy stood behind Lily and cleared his throat. No one so much as glanced in his direction. He tapped her on the shoulder. "Lily?"

She turned and looked at him like she had been expecting this. She gave a little smirk. "Hi, Tommy. I suppose you want to talk."

"Just for a second. I promise."

She turned back to her friends and said, "I'll be right back."

They walked over next to the wall, away from prying ears. "What could this possibly be about, Tommy?" Lily asked sarcastically, but then blushed.

"Look, I'm not even supposed to be talking to you. But, you have to tell me how long you've known," Tommy let out in a rush.

"You mean how long have I known about your incredible ability to turn into a gigantic cat whenever you want to?"

Tommy nodded quickly and nervously. He looked around to make sure no one was close enough to hear what she had said.

"I started putting things together a little after those guys broke into the museum. My dad started acting weird and that Asim guy came around. I got suspicious."

"I don't suppose you also know the reason I can do all of this, do you?" Tommy asked.

"I dunno. Because your dad could do it?"

"Something like that." Tommy was relieved. It was one thing that Lily knew he could turn into a cat. But if she found out he had descended from an Egyptian god, that was something entirely different.

"So what are you going to do? I mean, you can't tell anyone . . ."

"Oh, I know that. I wouldn't dare." She smiled and Tommy's heart melted. Then her expression changed, and her voice became quieter. "Actually, I was sort of hoping . . . to join you. To help you, or whatever."

Tommy's heart went from melting to nearly exploding. "You what?"

"I mean, if you wouldn't mind. You, Burt, your cousin . . . you guys are doing something to protect the world, and that just seems so . . . brave, I guess."

"Well," Tommy stalled. "I'd have to talk it over with them. We're a team, and—"

"Oh!" she blurted, and looked to the ground. "Of course. I know you guys probably wouldn't want me. I mean, I can't change into any cool animals or anything, but still . . ."

"Um, I'll bring it up to them, I guess." Tommy felt like he was in way over his head. The prettiest, nicest girl in school wanted to hang out with him and his friends? Lily had been somewhat friendly for the past few months, but now she almost seemed nervous to talk to him.

She glanced over her shoulder. "Look, I should get back. Let me know what they say, okay?"

Tommy turned and walked in the opposite direction. He felt like he was walking on clouds, like nothing could possibly go wrong. And then he slammed into a wall.

"Hey, Freak! Haven't seen you around in a while! You haven't been hiding from me, have

27

you?" Derrik Jackson smiled as Tommy gasped air back into his lungs. Derrik's partner in stupidity, Shawn Smart, patted the top of Tommy's head. Tommy swatted his hand away.

"What's the matter with you, Freak?" Derrik said. "What did you steal from Lily to lure her over here with you?"

"Leave me alone, Derrik," Tommy sighed. "I don't have time for this."

Derrik stepped closer and cast a shadow over Tommy. Tommy rolled his eyes. A lot had changed in the past few months. His recent experiences had turned his paralyzing fear of these two bullies into minor annoyance. But Derrik and Shawn hadn't picked up on Tommy's new opinion of them.

"I think he's gonna cry, Derrik," Shawn said.

"We can't have that, now can we? No, I think we'll just have to hit him until he feels better." Derrik took a step forward, his fists ready.

"That doesn't even make sense," Tommy muttered. He turned a foot to the door, ready to take off if he needed to.

"I wouldn't do that, Caveman," Annie said coolly. She and Burt were standing a few feet away with their arms crossed and game faces on.

Derrik and Shawn looked at each other, and burst out laughing. Annie shrugged. "Giggle if you want, ladies. But I bet you won't be laughing when word gets out that you got your rumps kicked by a girl half your size."

Derrik looked at Tommy. "I like your cousin, Bomani. She's hilarious. Too bad you're still gonna be dead meat the next time I see you outside of school." Shawn and Derrik walked away laughing, making sure they bumped Tommy as they passed.

Annie, Burt, and Tommy watched the two bullies knock a boy's tray to the ground on their way out of the cafeteria.

"Why do you still let them do that, Tommy?" Annie asked.

"Believe me, if I could convince them to leave me alone without having to go all shape-shifter on them, I'd do it in a heartbeat," said Tommy.

"Why were you talking to Lily?" Annie asked. "Making sure she keeps her mouth shut?"

"Uh, yeah, basically," Tommy muttered and ran his hand through his hair. "Actually, I was hoping to talk to you guys about something—"

Ms. Federline, the school secretary, interrupted him. "Thomas Bomani?" she asked Burt. "Your uncle called and left a note for you. Here."

"Um, actually, that's me," said Tommy.

Uncle? Tommy wondered. *I don't have an uncle.* He took the paper from Ms. Federline nonetheless. "Thank you, Ms. F."

Tommy waited for her to leave the lunchroom before opening the note. A puzzled expression appeared on his face.

"It's from Asim. He says to hurry to the warehouse right after school. And not to worry about telling our parents, since he's already called them."

"That's it? He lied to the school just to get us to training earlier? It doesn't say anything else?" Annie asked.

Tommy paused, sure he wasn't reading it correctly. "It says there's been another break-in at the museum."

CHAPTER 6

A Frightening Sign

"What did they take?" Burt asked.

Burt, Tommy, and Annie sat in the middle of the warehouse on the large, blue gym mats they used for hand-to-hand combat training. They were facing Asim, who was sitting on a folding chair. Detective Matthews was pacing the cement floor.

Asim responded, "As far as we can tell, nothing."

"These people walked right past priceless artifacts that would have suited any other thief," Detective Matthews said. "They went straight to an unmarked storage closet in the basement."

"But why?" Burt asked.

"Because it wasn't actually a storage closet. It was an ultra-secure safe disguised as a storage closet. And because this thief was attempting to take something he had come close to stealing before," Asim said softly.

"It was Fisk," Tommy said. His first instinct had been to blame Fisk, but he had hoped he was wrong. Now he saw how foolish that hope had been. His enemy had returned.

"We're fairly certain, yes," Detective Matthews said. "He left something of a sign to make sure we knew it was him who had been there. He found an Egyptian statue of the goddess Bastet and smashed the head."

Tommy gulped. Bastet was the mother of the original Bomani warrior. Only someone as arrogant as Fisk would make such a bold message.

Annie cut in, "He was *trying* to steal the piece, or he *did* steal the piece?"

"Fortunately, that section of the statue had been removed from the museum a few days before. It was only being held there temporarily, on its way to a more secure location," said Asim.

"Where is it now?" Tommy asked.

"It's safe," Detective Matthews said. "It's not here, but it's close enough for us to keep an eye on."

"Asim," Tommy started, but Asim cut him off.

"Tommy, if I knew where it is, you would know. For security's sake, the only people who know the piece's location are Detective Matthews and Curator Walker."

Tommy pressed his palms to his forehead. He had hoped for more time before having to find the next piece. The memory of being tricked into leading Fisk and his men right to a piece of the statue still burned fresh. He couldn't afford to let Badru acquire any more of the statue.

"What do we do, Asim?" Burt asked. "How do we keep Fisk from finding out where the new hiding place is and stealing it from there?"

Then Tommy got an idea. He knew what he needed to do. "We don't try to stop him," Tommy said, and everyone turned toward him. "Keeping that piece safe is important, but it's more important that we worry about moving forward."

"What are you talking about? Trying to find another fragment of the statue?" Annie asked.

"Exactly," Tommy said. "Fisk isn't afraid of us. He's going to keep hunting that piece until he gets it. We need to go after a different piece while he's distracted."

"But Tommy," Burt said, puzzled, "do we even know where another piece is?"

33

"I think one of us does." Tommy turned to his mentor. "Asim, how do we find the piece my father discovered the night he died?"

Asim smiled bitterly. "Tommy, I'm afraid you might be correct. But finding that piece is impossible. I'm sorry."

"How could it be impossible? Defending that statue is my family's job, and—"

Asim cut him off again. "Tommy, let me tell you a story. Something that didn't seem important until now."

"A story? But—"

"Trust me, Tommy, it is relevant to your worries." Asim closed his eyes in concentration.

"Your father's final battle took place very near here, in a place called the Flora Fields. The fight lasted hours. Each side used every bit of tooth, claw, and magic they could muster. Afterward, your mother found Husani on her doorstep, near death. He could barely move. He didn't even have the strength to speak."

Detective Matthews cleared his throat. "Tommy, Husani fought very hard against Badru that day. Badru nearly died. We think that may

be the reason he has been in hiding since then. When the—"

A knock on the door interrupted them. Seeing Lily Walker in the doorway made Tommy and Burt catch their breath.

"Do you mind if I come in?" Lily asked.

"No, Lily, of course not." Asim stood and motioned her to the center of the room. "I'm glad you could come. Your father must have delivered my message."

"He did."

"Good." He turned to the others. "I think Ms. Walker's surprise appearance the other day showed initiative and a talent for investigating. We'd be lucky to have that talent in this group."

Burt spoke up, his cheeks flushed, "I think it's a great idea. Welcome aboard, Lily."

"Thanks."

Tommy sighed in relief. He hadn't yet brought up the possibility of Lily joining them, afraid of how the others might react. Now he didn't have to.

"Back to less desirable things," Asim said, the hint of a smile fading from his face. "Please continue, Detective."

Detective Matthews began again, "Your father was exhausted by the battle with Badru and his men. As he was escaping with the statue, I assume he knew he wasn't going to live. He couldn't risk passing it to your mother without knowing he would be there to protect her, so he hid it."

"But you don't know where?" Burt asked.

"We have some ideas. Guesses," Asim said.

"Guesses give us something to work from, right? Fisk is distracted with finding the other statue fragment. So, we can look around all we want until we find this one." Tommy was becoming animated now, ready for action.

"I'm afraid that isn't an option, Tommy," said Asim. "Badru likely believes that we know exactly where the piece is. Now that we know Fisk is in town, moving anywhere near the Flora Fields would be too risky. Badru would certainly change his plans if it seemed we knew where more of the statue was."

"And even then, we might not be in the correct spot," Detective Matthews added.

"Why are you so unsure of where Husani hid it? How many places could there be?" Annie asked.

"Not many. A handful at most," Detective Matthews said.

Asim looked to Tommy. "Think back to Florida. What did you notice about the lake that was holding the statue?"

Annie took a guess, "It never aged and was always beautiful? That's why people thought it was the Fountain of Youth."

Asim nodded. "Exactly. Because of the statue's powers to propel life. A tribe of native Floridians once guarded that fragment. The piece we are looking for here was kept by a band of Celtic warriors in Ireland. When their descendants immigrated to America, they brought it with them. One of their people eventually died and was buried with their part of the statue."

Asim continued, "Husani was able to locate it because the small field in which that woman was buried was forever covered in flowers. Even in winter, under a foot of snow, beautiful flowers of every color grew as if it were the middle of summer."

"My father grew up by the Flora Fields," Lily said timidly. "He used to take us on picnics there when I was little. He told us about the flowers, about how they used to grow there all the time. But now they're all gone."

"That's right," Detective Matthews said. "Without the statue there, it's just a normal field."

Asim spoke up, "We had hoped we could find where Husani hid the piece by the area surrounding it—"

Detective Matthews interjected, "There is a limited area he could have hidden it in. The only options are a farm, a pond, or a riverbank riddled with small caves. None of them have shown any signs of the supernatural. Lily, is there anything unusual in that area that you've noticed?"

Lily looked starry-eyed. She clearly hadn't expected to be asked to contribute already. "I—I don't know. There's nothing weird I can think of. I mean, there just isn't a lot there. I think my dad said that the fishing is really good in that pond. Could that be something?"

Tommy ran his hands through his hair and tried to think. "Asim, if we don't know where the piece is and we can't go look for it, then what do we do?"

Asim sighed. "That is a question for your young minds, I'm afraid. I have been searching for this particular piece for over a decade, and I have no better idea where it is than when I started."

Dreams

Tommy laughed and took another long slurp of lemonade. He patted Annie on the back and then bumped his shoulder into Burt playfully. Lily followed behind the other three shyly. The crew was at the mall, taking some well-earned time off from training.

For the first time in weeks, Tommy felt completely at ease. He was happy he could just be Tommy for a little while, not Tommy Bomani: Savior of the World. Stumbling around the mall was the perfect remedy for his new responsibilities.

Tommy rolled his eyes as the girls peeled off to the side and into a chic clothing store. They couldn't afford anything in there, but that didn't stop them from looking around.

Tommy and Burt followed and complained about how bored they were. There was nothing Tommy hated more than shopping.

Burt yelled Tommy's name. Tommy turned back toward him, but then paused halfway.

He shook his head. *No way,* he thought. *No way he's that stupid.*

Tommy tried to listen to Burt, but then it happened again. Out of the corner of his eye, Tommy caught a flash of a man dressed in a dark business suit. A tall man with long, dark hair.

Was *Marcellus Fisk* walking around the *mall?*

Tommy ran out of the clothing store, leaving a confused Burt behind him. He ran in the direction he had last seen the man. He fought the urge to shift into something a little more catlike. His eyes had to be playing tricks.

But then he saw him.

Standing with hands on hips, facing Tommy without a trace of surprise on his face. Fisk smiled, and began slowly, arrogantly walking closer.

That was when Tommy realized he couldn't move.

He couldn't budge one muscle in his body, no matter how hard he tried. Only his eyes were free to move. They revealed that there wasn't just one Fisk, but dozens of them. They crowded him from all sides, slowly closing in like a smothering wave.

Tommy focused all his concentration on turning into a cat and fighting back. He wanted to teach the ghouls around him that the Bomanis couldn't be intimidated.

But it didn't matter what he wanted. The frightening figures were inching closer, whispering two words over and over: "I'm coming. I'm coming. I'm coming."

The next thing Tommy knew, he was lifting his sweat-covered head from the ground next to his bed. While fighting to move in his nightmare, he'd fallen in a tangle of sheets. He was breathing heavily, the image of Marcellus Fisk still burning in his brain.

Tommy wiped a strand of long hair from his eyes, then glanced at the bright red numbers on his alarm clock. It was six o'clock in the morning. On a Saturday.

He knew it took a lot of work to fight the forces of evil, but did it have to come so early in the morning?

CHAPTER 8

Readying

Tommy jumped in a somersaulting roll along the ground and into the shadows. He stayed on one knee and looked around. To his left was an uneven stack of five or six large tires, blocking his view. To the right was the edge of the wall, a perfect corner for a frontal attack. He was trapped. Thinking quickly he scrambled to the top of the tire pile.

Lily came around the corner seconds later. She gripped her paintball gun nervously, like she was afraid it would try to get away from her. She crouched low and swung her head and the barrel of the gun slowly side-to-side.

Tommy dropped to the ground as silently as he could, directly behind her. She didn't notice. Tommy smiled and wrapped her in a bear hug.

"Gotcha," he said playfully in her ear.

"Wha—? No!" Lily bellowed. "How did you do that?"

Asim's voice echoed through the warehouse, "Next station, Tommy."

Tommy left Lily behind and ran to the middle of the training center. There, Burt was standing on a corner of the blue mat. He had full sparring pads on his head, hands, and feet. He popped in a mouth guard and motioned Tommy into the makeshift ring.

Tommy stepped onto his corner of the mat and turned to Burt. They bowed to each other deeply from the waist. Then, each assumed a fighting stance.

The size difference between the two was laughable, but you couldn't tell from Tommy's face. He kept his gaze locked on Burt's and slowly walked forward until they met in the middle of the square. Burt took a giant swing with his right arm, but Tommy ducked and rolled to the left. He quickly hopped back to his feet and faced his friend.

Burt swung with his right again, but pulled it back and instead followed through with his left hand. Tommy swerved beneath the combination and ended up behind his opponent. With mad abandon, he launched his whole body at the backs of Burt's knees and dropped him to the ground.

Tommy scrambled forward without wasting a moment and pinned his friend's neck in a professional headlock. He held it until he felt Burt's hand tap against his leg three times, signaling defeat.

He stood up and offered Burt a hand, which was taken with a smile. "Nice job, Tommy," Burt said sheepishly.

Asim's voice bounced through the loudspeaker once more. "Next station."

Two down, one to go. Tommy marched to the far end of the warehouse, where Annie was waiting for him. He took a deep breath and let it out as he shook her hand.

"Good luck, cousin," he said.

"You're going to need more than luck to win today, Tommy," she replied. "I've been practicing."

He smirked. "I hope you've been practicing losing gracefully, because there's no way I'm coming up short."

They each shifted into their animal forms. Standing in their places now were a shimmering, silver desert cat and a large, gnarly-haired dog. They placed their front paws on the yellow line before them and tensed their bodies.

Asim's voice exploded through the heavy air. "GO!"

Annie jumped to her right, blocking Tommy's path. He stumbled but quickly regained his footing.

So we're playing that way today, huh? he thought. *Well, you aren't the only one who wants to win.*

Tommy watched Annie cut left and bound up the steel steps toward the catwalk above. He decided on a shortcut. He ran straight ahead and leaped to the top of the tire pile he had used to fool Lily. This time, he treated them like a trampoline and jumped from the tires onto the catwalk.

He trotted to an old golden bell and rang it with a satisfied smirk. This signaled his completion of the first leg of the race.

Annie barreled around the corner of the stairway, furious her lead had been spoiled. The bell shook to the ground as she rumbled by it, intent on tracking down her tricky cousin.

Tommy bolted down the stairs at the far end of the catwalk and turned left. Then, he slowed almost to a stop. Twenty yards ahead of him sat the next bell, posted on top of a metal chair. All that stood between him and the bell was a sea of mousetraps, waiting to snap onto anything that dared touch them.

He weaved, dodged, and tiptoed to the best of his ability. He made his way through the first half of the traps untouched.

The sound of a bell sweetly ringing jolted his attention. His head jerked up and there stood Annie. She was in human form, the bell in her left hand and a rope in her right. Tommy now saw she had used it to swing down from the catwalk, avoiding the pit of mousetraps altogether.

Tommy gritted his teeth and bolted forward. He did his best to ignore the pain as trap after trap violently grasped his paws and tail.

Annie winked at him, then turned back into a dog and charged toward the final leg of the race. Tommy cleared the traps, which continued to snap after he had passed. He jumped to within a couple feet of Annie's shaggy tail.

The third leg of the race was an eight-foot-long, shallow pool of water. The one rule guiding it was simple: if you went in the water, your race was over.

Tommy saw Annie running as fast as she could, and he knew she meant to jump over the pool entirely. Usually Annie would try to figure out a way to sneak across, but she could taste victory.

Tommy knew what he had to do. If he was going to beat Annie, he had to take a risk. He ran as hard as he could until he was keeping pace alongside her.

He let her jump. Then he jumped . . . and landed on Annie's back. He used her as a stepping-stone to push himself across the water. He watched as she crashed into the water below him.

Annie landed with a bark and a splash as Tommy skidded up to the final bell. He turned back into his normal, undersized self and spun around to face his soaking-wet opponent.

He smiled as he rang the bell.

"Well done, Tommy!" Asim said as he came out of his office beaming. "I think you and Annie may have bent the rules during your race. But I doubt we can expect Badru to fight a clean battle."

Annie began laughing from the pool, where she pretended to swim in the shallow water. Burt and Lily walked up and stood on the edge.

"Jeez, Tommy! I know cats don't like water, but wasn't that taking things a little far?" Lily laughed.

Tommy continued to smile. "There was no way I was losing today."

47

Lily shrugged. "Yeah, well, we'll just see how next time goes. You can't mysteriously appear behind me every time."

"Soon all of you will run out of easy solutions," Asim said. "You'll have to think in ways you have never thought before. Our enemy has been up to his evil deeds for thousands of years. We must do our best to counter the advantage that Badru gains from his experience. We must think strategically, and—"

"Asim?" Tommy interrupted. "Are you using a lot of words to say that we need to think instead of just act?"

Asim paused before answering with, "Possibly."

"And is that going to eventually lead to these guys going home and me staying late to play you in backgammon?"

Asim smiled. "Most definitely."

Tommy nodded, unsurprised. "That's what I thought. The fun just never stops."

48

CHAPTER 9

A First

sim smiled at Tommy from across the backgammon board, hardly looking at the pieces he had just moved. Tommy felt himself blush under the unwavering gaze and began to laugh.

"Why are you smiling at me like that?" he finally asked.

Asim joined him in laughing.

"You are a very special boy, do you know that, Tommy?"

"Um . . . thank you?" Tommy rolled his dice. He thought for a moment, then shifted some pieces around the board. He took one of Asim's defeated soldiers and placed it on the rail.

Asim laughed again, harder this time.

"You remind me so much of your father sometimes. Like today, when you leaped onto Annie's back in midair to get across the puddle. That sort of creativity—it's a Bomani family trait that has helped keep this planet safe from evil people for a very long time."

Tommy shrugged. "I needed to get across. It seemed like a good solution to a sticky situation."

"To *you* it was a solution. To most people, it would have been an impossibility, a dream. You are becoming more like a warrior every day."

Tommy gave a half-smile. He fidgeted with the dice before tossing them back onto the board. He gritted his teeth and made a confession.

"Asim, I think someone was following me today."

Asim didn't look surprised. He calmly watched Tommy finish out his turn, then rolled the dice and moved his own pieces. After a silence that pressed on Tommy like a weight, he spoke again. "Who do you think was following you?"

"I can't be sure. It was just one man. He never got too close, but every time I turned around he was standing on the horizon."

"Did he see you come here?"

"To the warehouse?"

Asim nodded.

"I don't think so. I weaved around through some different neighborhoods and cut through the woods. I'm pretty sure I lost him."

"It's your turn, Tommy."

Tommy rolled the dice again and mentally measured the board. Asim stared into space.

"It would seem this is one of Badru's men," Asim said. "But if he does not know of this location, there's probably nothing to worry about. For now."

Tommy moved his pieces. "I thought the same thing. I'm sure Fisk is just trying to figure out what we're up to."

"That is likely a very good guess. But I want you to tell me if this continues, or if it gets worse. Badru has always used evil men for his dirty work, but Marcellus Fisk seems to be especially dangerous."

Asim rolled his dice and moved his soldier back onto the board. They both sat in silence for a moment, playing the game. Tommy was ahead, but he knew it was only a matter of time before Asim took control. He always did.

Asim spoke, and this time he did not smile. "Tommy, I am going to ask you a question. Please be honest in your response, for it is very important."

The dice stayed still in Tommy's hand, and he met his mentor's gaze. He nodded and brushed a dark strand of hair from his eyes.

"Are you afraid of Marcellus Fisk?"

Tommy looked down to the board and thought about the question. Somehow, this wasn't something he had ever considered. He wanted to make sure he answered correctly.

"I had a dream last night," he said, "where I was walking through the mall and Fisk appeared out of nowhere. But it wasn't just him. There were dozens of him, all the same, and all wanting to hurt me and take away my necklace."

Asim was intrigued. "What did you do?"

"I couldn't do anything. I couldn't move, even though I tried."

"But if you could have done something?"

Tommy looked back up and locked eyes with Asim. "I would have fought every one of them. I would have done everything I possibly could to protect this necklace."

Asim took in a deep breath, then he let it out. He nodded to the dice still in Tommy's hand. "Your turn, Tommy."

Tommy dropped the dice to the board. As he calculated his moves, his jaw dropped slightly. He passed his hand around the board and put the last of his pieces into their home slot.

"I won?" Tommy said. "Did I just win?"

Asim smiled again, but differently than he had before. Pride beamed through his eyes.

"And I lost," Asim said, "for the first time in thirty years."

CHAPTER 10

A Long Time Coming

Annie, Burt, and Lily dodged over and around sidewalk cracks as they made their way home. Burt pulled up the rear and Lily danced around ahead of them, walking backward as she talked.

"Really, Burt? You honestly think you can tell us your family got a puppy and expect us to not want to see it?"

"Yeah, what else do you have to do that you can't let us come over for a few minutes?" Annie asked.

"I've got homework," Burt said.

Lily stopped in her tracks and turned around as the other two passed by her. "Burt, it's Saturday! No one does homework on Saturday!"

Burt rubbed his arm nervously and looked to the sky. "Well . . . I do. And I have to, uh, clean my room, too. And wash my dad's car. Twice."

"Okay, that doesn't even make sense. Besides, Annie and I should come over so we can talk about, you know, saving the world stuff." Lily was clearly still excited about helping them out.

She continued, "I've been thinking a lot about where the statue piece could be."

"Whoa." Annie stopped walking and looked down the street at two familiar thugs throwing rocks at an abandoned house. "Sorry Lily, but you're going to have to hold that thought."

She smiled and turned back in the direction they had come from. "Okay, I'm sure Asim wouldn't approve, but those two dorks have given you guys nothing but grief for, like, forever."

Burt balked. "Annie, I don't—"

Annie held up a hand. "Burt, we owe this to Tommy. They need to be taught a lesson. Now, does that convenience store over there sell shaving cream or not?"

Crash! The remaining shards of an old window tumbled to the ground, destroyed by a golf ball-sized rock.

"Stupid house," Shawn muttered, then threw another stone. It put a dent in the building's siding.

"Yeah," Derrik agreed as he chucked a rock the size of his fist and sent a wooden shutter falling.

The boys had been standing in the same spot for nearly half an hour, throwing rocks and insulting anything they saw. When a squirrel ran across the building's front stoop, Derrik's rock missed it by a few feet. The squirrel slowly trotted off into the bushes.

"Stupid squirrel," Derrik said.

"Rabies!"

"What did you say, Shawn?"

"I didn't say nothin'," Shawn answered.

Derrik stopped throwing and looked at his friend. "If you didn't say that, then who did?"

The answer came from their left. Running toward them at a frightening speed were Burt and Lily, screaming for their lives.

"Rabies! It's got rabies!" Burt hollered.

"Look, Miller's gone nutty. And is that Lily with him? What is he yellin' about?"

"Run! It's got rabies! We're all gonna die!" Burt blasted straight between them, not stopping to explain. Lily followed close behind.

"Rabies!" she squeaked.

Both boys watched them run by, then looked back in the direction they had come from. Suddenly, Shawn began screaming like a tea kettle. The boys twisted back around and started sprinting, moving faster than they had ever dreamed possible.

Hot on their heels trailed a large, dark-haired dog with a mad look in its eyes. A thick stream of foam poured from its mouth.

"Rabies!" they yelled, and bounded in the opposite direction.

The boys began to gain on Burt. No matter how fast they ran, the dog always seemed to edge closer. They crossed streets without looking, but still they could do nothing to lengthen the gap.

On the edge of Portrait Oaks Park they passed Lily and Burt. Choosing between a lifelong friendship and a painful death, Derrik made what he considered an easy choice. He kicked Shawn in the leg, sending him to the ground hard.

Derrik peeked over his shoulder as he ran, hoping the wild animal would take the bait. He saw it leap over Shawn and pick up speed. Derrik could hear it growling as it gained on him, and he swore he could feel its diseased foam hitting his legs.

Tears now coursing down his cheeks, Derrik turned toward the Forbidden Oak. He ignored the first branch and leaped straight to the second. Derrik moved so frantically up the next two he didn't even feel the bark cutting his hands. Without looking down, he scaled past the fifth and sixth branches and continued climbing.

After a few more branches, Derrik made a final leap no one in their right mind would consider. He grabbed a branch barely thick enough to hold a boy half his size and hung by his fingertips.

Sweaty, exhausted, and crying, he gripped as hard as he could. He searched the branches below him and then the ground. There was no dog to be seen. He had escaped!

"Hey, Derrik," came a voice from below. "What are you doing up there?"

Standing at the base of the tree were Annie, Lily, and Burt. Annie turned away and yelled to a group of kids playing four square across the playground.

"Hey, guys! Come check this out!"

"Miller, where did it go?" Derrik yelled.

The gaggle of classmates made their way over and stood next to the tree.

"Where did what go?" Burt asked.

"The dog!"

"What are you talking about?"

"The dog with rabies, stupid!"

Annie turned and said something Derrik couldn't hear. Everybody began to laugh.

"Hey, he broke Tommy's record," a boy said.

"I guess he did," Lily responded. "Congratulations, Derrik. How's your grip?"

His grip was not good. "All of you are gonna be hurtin', even the girls!"

Burt laughed, a little nervous but comforted by how far Derrik would have to fall to run after him. "Really? And are you going to come down here, or would you like us to go up there?"

Derrik had no response. He looked around for Shawn, but his friend was nowhere to be seen.

"You know what, I think we're fine without a beating for now. You have fun up there, though, okay?" Burt and the girls moved away from the group.

Someone said, "Rabies!" and everyone began to laugh. The group walked back to their game. Derrik was left alone, the new record holder of the Forbidden Oak.

CHAPTER 11

Where There's Smoke . . .

Tommy felt like he was floating over the cracked cement sidewalk as he made his way home. He still couldn't believe he had beaten Asim at backgammon.

After he had returned from Florida, all he'd wanted to do was train. He wanted to eliminate any advantage Fisk would have the next time they met. Asim wanted the same thing.

Losing a battle so early in the war had lit a fire in Asim. From then on, everything Tommy did was watched closely.

Asim had agreed to tell Tommy everything he knew about the Bomanis of the past. In exchange, Tommy had agreed to elevating their readying sessions to more challenging heights.

Asim covered every aspect of battle in their training, even those that affected Tommy's fights indirectly. He helped Tommy realize how knowing about his godly heritage affected how he viewed his abilities. Tommy now knew he had a responsibility to honor the work done by everyone who had ever opposed Badru.

Asim ran every training session with more intensity than the one before. After a few days, Tommy began to rise to the challenge. Every day Asim would present him with new obstacles. Tommy would think his way around them with increasing ease. And now he had defeated Asim in backgammon! Even Burt hadn't been able to do that.

Tommy shuffled his feet in a little dance and looked up toward the setting sun. Birds chirped and a light breeze brushed against his skin. The smell of acrid smoke worked its way into his nostrils.

The smoke woke his brain from its daydream and dragged him back to the real world. *What's burning?* Tommy thought. He pulled in a deeper whiff.

He looked back toward the horizon and found his answer. Half a block away, black smoke was pouring through the open windows of a house.

Tommy bolted into the house's front yard and glanced around. There were no fire trucks or worried neighbors calling for help.

No one else has seen the fire, Tommy realized. Suddenly a burst of orange flame jumped behind a second-story window as its drapes were engulfed.

With a deep breath, Tommy ignored everything he had ever learned in fire safety class and ran toward the front door.

Wisps of dark smoke twirled through the crack of the open door. Tommy gave it a swift kick and dropped back a step. He tucked his face into the front of his T-shirt to fight the clouds of smoke that escaped the house. Then, he moved inside.

What he saw was more frightening than his worst nightmares. Flames danced over every bit of carpet, furniture, and wood. They destroyed everything in their path. He shuffled forward.

Within seconds, Tommy couldn't see a thing. The smoke made his eyes water, and he began coughing as the oxygen around him disappeared. His foot caught on a heavy object and he fell to the ground.

He landed next to a motionless man, who was cut and bleeding. Tommy recognized the man instantly. It was Lily's father. This was Lily's house.

Tommy's eyes widened and he spun around. The door was less than ten feet away. He couldn't risk shifting and having his fur catch on fire. He would have to do this the hard way.

Tommy dropped down and grabbed Mr. Walker under both armpits. He planted his sneakers on the linoleum floor and pushed. He slowly pulled the much larger man along with him toward the door.

Tommy planted his feet and pushed again. His vision began to blur, but they had moved another foot.

Push, pull, stop. Push, pull, stop. Every time Tommy repeated the process his body told him it couldn't do another. But he knew he had to.

A flaming glob of melted paint fell from the ceiling, landing just to the side of Tommy. A fire alarm dropped violently where Mr. Walker had been just moments before.

Finally Tommy felt clean air wash over his face. With one more pull, Mr. Walker's head was outside as well.

"There's a kid in there!" someone yelled from the street. Seconds later Tommy was pulled down onto the lawn. He watched as two men pulled Mr. Walker onto the grass next to him. Tommy turned over onto his knees and leaned over Mr. Walker.

"Mr. Walker?" he asked gently. "Mr. Walker, wake up."

Tommy heard an ambulance and a fire truck roar into the street behind them. He ignored them. "Mr. Walker," he tried again. "You're safe now."

Mr. Walker's eyes fluttered partway open. He looked to Tommy and mouthed the two words Tommy knew were coming: "Marcellus Fisk."

Tommy stood and moved to the side as an ambulance worker began moving Mr. Walker onto a stretcher.

Tommy waved off an offer of help from a medic. He started walking back toward the warehouse. Soon, his walk turned into a run. He had to tell Asim.

Fisk had moved beyond stealing from museums and sneaking through jungles. He was making house calls. It was anyone's guess how far he would go before he was stopped.

CHAPTER 12

Too Much

Some people hate the way hospitals smell. Tommy hated the way hospitals sound. Everything is always overwhelmingly still and quiet, unless something is going wrong.

Right now, though, he was okay with everything being quiet. Mr. Walker had managed to get away with a few minor cuts, bruises, and burns. He had no permanent injuries.

Tommy looked into Mr. Walker's room through a window in the hall. The door was shut, but he knew what Mr. Walker was telling Asim and his wife and daughter. He was telling them how Fisk had left him to die.

Tommy had just finished telling Burt and Annie how he had been followed on his way to the warehouse earlier in the morning. Then he told them how he had noticed the fire.

Asim emerged from the room and shut the door behind him. He pulled Tommy, Annie, and Burt over into a corner and whispered the news.

"I'm afraid there is no doubt. Fisk and his men trapped Mr. Walker. They tried to torture him to get information about the statue piece. When he wouldn't tell them where it was, they hit him over the head and started a fire. If you hadn't been passing by, Tommy . . ."

"What do we do now, Asim?" Tommy asked.

"The Walkers will be leaving town as soon as Mr. Walker is cleared to leave the hospital. I have called your parents and suggested they do the same, Burt. Of course, if you want to go with them . . ."

"Not a chance." Burt's jaw clenched. "Lily is our friend. I'm here to help."

Tommy stared at his friend with admiration. Burt hadn't been this worked up when Fisk had nearly killed him two months ago. It was hard not to match his determination.

Asim pulled a handkerchief from his pocket and wiped his forehead. He had a worried expression Tommy had never seen him wear before. It was unlike Asim to appear anything but utterly composed. Mr. Walker was Asim's good friend, and the attack had apparently shaken him.

"He has indeed gone too far," Asim said. He pointed to Tommy's mother and aunt, who were sitting across the hall from Mr. Walker's door.

They were holding each other's hand and talking seriously.

"Annie and Tommy," Asim continued, "your mothers are still undecided about what they will do. Naturally, Kirsten wants to stay and help you fight. But I think the wisdom of caution will win, and they may find a place less visible for the time being."

"Maybe they could go with my family," Burt suggested.

"An excell—" Asim's face suddenly tightened, and he looked confused. A gasp escaped as he clutched at his chest. He started to fall, but Burt caught him and placed him carefully on the ground. Tommy grabbed a towel from a cart in the hall and balled it up under Asim's neck, creating a makeshift pillow.

"Somebody help!" Annie yelled. "Get a doctor!"

Tommy grabbed Asim's hand and held it tight. His mouth gaped open. Asim's eyes darted back and forth and began to close.

Tommy had never been so afraid in his life.

CHAPTER 13

A Brave Gift

Two hours later, Tommy stood outside of Asim's hospital room, but he couldn't go in. In the short time he had known Asim, he had only thought of his mentor as invincible. To see him lying in a hospital bed, barely conscious, would absolutely destroy that image.

Burt placed his arm around his friend. "He's gonna be okay, Tommy. I mean he's already, what, a hundred years old? One little heart attack can't stop him."

Tommy forced a smile, but he didn't laugh.

"Tommy," Burt began, his forehead crinkled in thought. "Do you think the statue piece that was in the museum is nearby? Do you think Mr. Walker knows where it is?"

Tommy shook his head. "He said Detective Matthews put it somewhere without telling him. That's why he couldn't tell Fisk where it was even if he had wanted to. Why?"

"Well, the piece has life-generating powers, right? So maybe if Asim had the piece with him,

68

or near him, it would help him get through his heart attack. I mean, that could work, right?"

Tommy nodded his head slowly. "You're probably right. I wish we knew where it was. Annie, have you been able to get Detective Matthews on the phone?"

Annie shook her head no quickly. "And I tried, like, a hundred times."

"But that's a really good thought, Burt," Tommy said. "Really good."

"Hi, guys," Lily said as she walked up behind them. Her parents had moved out of the room and were now in the hall, watching. Mr. Walker was wearing a few large bandages and was sitting in a wheelchair, but Tommy knew that was just because it was hospital policy. Annie gave Lily a hug.

"How's your dad?" Annie asked.

"He's good. Not great, but good." Lily smiled weakly. "He's a lot better than he would have been if Tommy hadn't saved him."

"Isn't that the truth," Burt said softly. None of them wanted to think about what would have happened if Tommy hadn't noticed that smoke.

"So, my parents are leaving, if you want to say good-bye," Lily said.

Annie looked at her, confused. "You mean you're leaving. I thought—"

Lily shook her head. "I'm staying. There's got to be some way I can help you find the people that burned my house down."

"Your parents are okay with that?" Burt asked.

"I don't think I've ever seen my dad so proud of anything I've ever said."

"That's great!" Burt yipped, and wrapped Lily up in a giant bear hug. Realizing what he had done, he quickly set her back on the ground and backed away. His entire face was now as red as a strawberry. "I mean, your assistance is very much appreciated."

Mrs. Bomani and Aunt Kirsten came out of Asim's room. They turned to the kids, their faces ashen and tired.

Mrs. Bomani spoke, "We're going to leave now, kids. And we think it would be best if we got a hotel room for a couple of nights, just in case."

"It isn't likely Fisk would come for us, but if he did . . . well, we'd rather be safe than sorry," Kirsten finished.

Tommy and Annie walked up to their mothers and gave them hugs. Then they switched and hugged their aunts. Burt and Lily took their turns next. By the end, both women had tears in their eyes.

"Where are you four going to stay?" Mrs. Bomani asked.

"Sorry, Mrs. B," Burt said. "We've decided it would be best if you didn't know. For safety's sake."

The mothers nodded in understanding. Tommy wondered how they could completely trust four kids to defend them against such terrible evil. It took a lot of faith.

"You just be safe, okay?" Mrs. Bomani said. "And make Asim proud." Tommy nodded slowly.

"Guys, why don't you walk these two to their car. I've got to see Asim for a second before we go," Tommy said.

Tommy's mom kissed him on the cheek. Then, she looked him over for what seemed like forever. At Burt's gentle insistence, she turned and followed the rest of the group toward the hospital's exit.

Tommy walked into Asim's room. It was completely still but for the flickering of a muted television. The silence made him uneasy.

Asim was lying on his back, propped against a pillow. His eyes were open, but barely. Their usual blue had diminished to a dull gray, but they still held a bit of their mystical glisten.

Asim held out his hand, and Tommy took it. For a moment they said nothing. Then Tommy reached to his own neck and pulled off his necklace. Ra's statue shimmered in the dull florescent lighting as he placed the chain over Asim's head.

"Right now you need this more than I do," Tommy whispered. "It'll help you get strong again."

Tommy took his hand again and squeezed it. He tried to turn away to leave, but Asim held him firm.

"Tommy," he said, "if it comes to it you must kill Fisk. He is too dangerous." Asim paused and took a breath, then started again. "Without him, Badru will be helpless, hidden in the desert."

Tommy replied, "I will do whatever it takes to protect the Sun of Ra."

Asim's face never moved, but his eyes smiled. "You couldn't be more like your father if you tried. Good luck, Tommy."

CHAPTER 14

Change of Direction

The taxi rolled to a stop across the street from Tommy's house. Tommy stepped out from the front passenger seat. He paused and then sat back down, shutting the door behind him. He stared straight ahead without saying a word.

Finally Annie couldn't take it anymore. "What are you doing? Why did you get back in?"

Tommy slammed his hand against the dashboard. Burt and the girls pulled back, even more confused. Tommy looked at the cab driver, and then at his friends.

"Guys, can I talk to you outside?"

They all stepped out of the car and moved toward Tommy. He pointed across the street to his house. "The door is open. He left it open."

Burt's eyes went wide. "Fisk is here?"

"He is, or he was. I can feel it," Tommy shook his head. Frustration was twisting his stomach into a knot. Fisk was becoming more aggressive. He kept trying to end their next fight before it even started, and Tommy was a step behind every time.

"But why would he come here? The men following you had to have let him know you weren't home," Lily said.

"Exactly. After he couldn't get any answers out of your dad, he probably thought he'd have better luck with my mom and Aunt Kirsten. He knew I wouldn't be here to protect them."

Tommy stared at Annie. "I bet our moms left for the hospital just a couple of minutes before he got here."

"Then let's go get him!" Annie said. She and Tommy started around the car, but Burt grabbed them both by the arm.

"No!" Burt said. "Think about this. Why would he leave the door open? He wants you to know that he was here. He's trying to let you know that you weren't able to stop him from going into your house."

Lily nodded, following Burt's train of thought. "But if he is still in there, he probably set a trap. He left the door open so you would come barging in after him."

"Exactly," Burt said. "For all we know there are fifty guys with Fisk in there, ready to grab us as soon as we walk in."

"Who cares?" Annie barked. "Tommy and I can take on a hundred of them, if—"

"Burt and Lily are right," Tommy said. "There's no point in going in there, not now. We're going to have to confront Fisk eventually, but we can't give him the upper hand again. We can't give him the chance to set another trap."

"Then what're we going to do?" Annie asked.

"We're gonna go to the warehouse, just like we'd planned," Tommy said. "We were only coming here to grab extra blankets and stuff anyway. We can make due without them for a night or two if we need to."

"But what about bikes? How are we going to get anywhere if we don't take our bikes?" Lily asked. "We can't just keep taking cabs everywhere."

Tommy spoke up. "I have an extra bike at the warehouse. I don't think we'll really need them though. The Flora Fields are only a mile or two from the warehouse."

"Tommy, you heard what Asim said about that. If we go anywhere near those fields, we'll have an

75

army of Badru's men on us in a second," Burt said, shaking his head.

Tommy shrugged. "Then maybe that's what we have to do. I'd rather go right at Fisk than shadow behind him like an annoying ghost. Maybe we can trick them."

"We'll figure out what we're going to do about Fisk once we're at the warehouse," Burt said. "When we're sure we haven't been followed. Okay?"

"Sounds good to me."

Burt opened the passenger door and spoke to driver. "Sir, would it be okay if you drove us a couple more miles down the road? We'd like to go somewhere different."

The man took a good look at Burt, and then at the other three behind him. "Aren't you kids a bit young to be riding around town in cabs and worrying about things?"

Tommy stepped forward. "Mister, if you only knew half of what we're dealing with right now, all you'd be worried about is where we need to go and how fast we need to get there."

"Do you have enough money?"

Lily pulled out the cab money her father had given her earlier. He had said it was the least he could do to thank Tommy for saving his life.

"Then quit wasting time and climb back in. Sounds like you have some work to do."

The kids jumped back inside the car. The driver pushed down the gas pedal, leaving a cloud of burned rubber and dust behind them.

The driver laughed. "Jeez, the hurry you kids are in, you'd think you were trying to save the world."

CHAPTER 15

Silhouettes

Tommy raised his palm toward the other three at the warehouse door, stopping them where they stood. They had left the cab behind a few hundred yards down the road. Tommy hoped their early exit and detour through a small patch of forest was enough to lose anyone following them.

"Annie, you and I are going in first. You two wait here. We'll be right back."

Burt nodded and pulled the door open. Annie and Tommy transformed and slowly crept inside, their ears pointed forward and their noses sniffing the air around them.

Lily looked around nervously. She had appeared confident and almost excited up until now. Burt had forgotten that she wasn't as battle-tested as the rest of them.

"You seem kind of distracted. How are you?"

She shrugged. "I'm doing okay, I guess. I mean, I'm not scared, if that's what you're thinking."

"Good," Burt said. "What's on your mind?"

She walked next to the door and leaned back against the steel wall. "I can't stop wondering where the statue piece might be. It seems like the answer should be in my brain somewhere. I just can't track it down.

"My grandparents used to take my dad there when he was little, back when it was still pretty. He liked to take us on picnics all over that area when I was a kid, even though all the flowers were gone. Mom and I would set up the food, and he would go on these long walks . . . ," Lily trailed off, and then burst out laughing.

Burt started laughing a little, not sure if he had missed something funny.

"Oh, Burt!" Lily chuckled, then caught her breath and slowed down. "My dad wasn't going on walks. He was looking for the statue piece!"

"I bet you're right. He probably took you on those picnics so he could poke around. I guess being in the Protectorate isn't a part-time job."

"Burt, have you ever—" Lily froze. She looked up toward the horizon.

"What is it?" Burt followed her gaze. Then, he instinctively placed his body in front of Lily's.

Standing on the horizon were three men.

"Oh no," Burt moaned.

The door slipped open next to them. Tommy stepped out. "All's clear, folks. Hello? Hey guys, what're you—"

Burt shoved him inside, and pulled Lily along with him. He slammed the door shut and turned every lock he could find.

"Burt, what's the big idea?" Tommy asked.

"Whatever we're gonna do next, Tommy, we gotta do it fast," Burt blurted out. "We just saw three guys standing on the top of the hill."

Lily joined in. "Fisk found us!"

Annie put her hands on Lily's shoulders. "Calm down, Lily. How do you know they were Fisk's men? It could have just been three dudes out for a walk."

Burt cleared his throat then authoritatively said, "I recognized all three from the Fountain of Youth. We need a plan and quick."

"Burt, all we need right now is for Annie and I to go out there and shut those three down. If they don't get back to Fisk, then he doesn't know where we are," Tommy nearly yelled.

"Tommy, calm down." Burt forced Tommy to look into his eyes. "Chances are those were only the three we saw. I'd bet another one has already run to tell Fisk."

Tommy threw his hands up in the air. He paced, transforming back and forth between a boy and a house cat. Although he was glad he had given his necklace to Asim, he still felt slightly out of sorts without it. He had grown accustomed to being a powerful large cat, but he couldn't achieve that form without the necklace.

"Well, what are we going to do? Just sit here and wait for them to attack us?" Annie asked.

"No!" Tommy said. "We need to figure out where my dad hid the statue piece and get it."

"But we don't have any idea where it is," Burt reasoned.

"I don't know then. We've got to think about the places Asim said it might be. What were they?" Tommy put his hands in his hair.

Annie snapped her fingers, trying to fire her brain into remembering. "It was a pond, a farm, or some caves. That's what he said."

"Why can't I figure this out?" Lily yelled.

"Lily, don't worry about it. None of us can think of it right now. But it'll come," Annie said.

"You don't understand," Lily said. "I've been to all of those places, like, a million times. I know I know the answer, but it just won't come to me. I just wish that I—" Lily's jaw dropped and her eyes lit up. The other three stopped and looked at her.

"Lily?" Burt asked. "You okay?"

Lily's dazed eyes turned slowly and locked with Burt's. Then she began dancing and jumping around, laughing like a crazy person. "The well!" she shouted.

Tommy looked to Burt, who returned his confused expression. "Lily? What well?"

"The wishing well!" she yelled, and then ran up and hugged each of the three in turn. "On the farm there was this old well that I liked to throw pennies into. Sometimes when I did I would make wishes."

"So? What does that have to do with you acting like you've lost your mind?" Tommy asked.

"Because every time I did, my wish came true!" Lily smiled. She had finally stopped jumping around, but her smile was as large as ever.

"Like what?" Annie asked.

"Like when I was sick and my dad took me on

a picnic to make me feel better. As soon as I dropped a penny in that well and wished I felt better, I went completely back to normal."

Burt tilted his head and looked at her, thinking. "What else, Lily?"

"One time, I got to visit the animals on the farm. There was a horse that had just broken its leg and they said they were going to have to put it down. But a little bit after I made a wish, the horse was just fine. In fact, he lived for years!"

"If the piece is somewhere in the well, it's using its powers to heal!" Burt said. "It's evidence of the statue's ability to enhance life."

"Lily, you did it!" Annie shrieked, and both girls danced in a circle.

"Awesome job, Lily," Tommy said. "Now tell me where that well is so I can get the piece out."

"Tommy, no!" Burt yelled. He took a deep breath, and when he started again his words were softer. "Rushing off to save the day is exactly what gave Fisk the advantage last time."

Tommy started to protest, but Burt cut him off with a quick hand movement. "I don't mean to shoot you down, but we need to do this right. I think I've got a plan, but it's a bit risky. I just hope we've got enough time."

CHAPTER 16

A New Plan

The warehouse door flew open and Tommy marched out, looking upset. He turned around the far corner, then returned on a mountain bike just as Burt, Lily, and Annie came outside.

"Tommy, what are you doing?" Lily asked.

"This is crazy," Annie added.

Loose gravel kicked from his tires as Tommy hit the brakes right in front of Burt. "Tommy, will you please just stop and think about what you're doing? This is unreasonable. What if we're wrong? What if that isn't where the statue piece is?" Burt pleaded.

"It's right, Burt, I know it is. I'm sorry you three don't want to come with me, but I'm sure this is the right thing to do," Tommy said. "We can't risk Fisk finding it before we do."

"So what happens if you do find it?" Burt yelled. He had lost his cool, and his powerful voice reminded those who had forgotten just how large he actually was. "What do you do then? Are you really going to watch Fisk steal another piece that we've worked to find? All you're doing is helping Badru gain power!"

Tommy looked back at Burt, shocked at the harshness of his tone. Tommy's voice came out soft, a perfect contrast to his booming friend. "I'm doing exactly what I'm supposed to do. I'm going to find the piece. Fisk can't stop me, and if he were here, Badru couldn't stop me, either."

Annie walked up to Tommy and gently grabbed his arm. "Please, Tommy. I want to go there as badly as you do, but we just aren't ready. Come back inside for a few minutes."

Tommy stood up on the pedals, ready to take off. "Sorry, guys. I just can't take the chance of losing another piece to Badru. If you want to help, you know where I'll be."

He pushed the bike forward and began pedaling as hard as he could, not even bothering to use the seat.

In a minute, Tommy was just a dot against the darkening horizon. Burt watched three familiar shapes step out of the woods and begin running in the direction Tommy had headed.

"They heard everything," Burt said. He stepped into the warehouse and waved for the girls to follow him. "Come on. We've got work to do."

Tommy pumped his legs, urging the bike to move faster. At the top of the hill he peeked back over his shoulder. He saw three men running to a car and a motorcycle parked near where he and his friends had left the taxi earlier that night.

Burt was right, he thought. *I recognize those three from Florida, too.* The thought sent a shiver down his spine.

The car's lights flipped on and pointed directly at Tommy. He gripped the handlebars and swerved his bike off the road and onto a sidewalk. The headlights still grew closer. Finally, the lights turned down a different road and were driving away from him.

They're going to tell Fisk, he realized.

The motorcycle trailed behind from a good distance, just a bobbing light cruising down the road. He wondered if the driver actually thought Tommy didn't know he was there.

Tommy pulled around a corner and realized he was already close to his destination. *If this doesn't work*, he caught himself, and changed his tone. *No, this will work. Badru can't gain another piece. That much more strength might be just what he needs to get his power back. Then nothing would stop him from coming after my family . . .*

Tommy shook the thought from his head. He looked to the side and realized he was riding past the Flora Fields. He was just a couple of miles from his house. Tommy had driven or walked past these fields hundreds of times without realizing what they were. He'd never known that these were the fields where his father had fought his last battle.

He looked behind him once more. The lone motorcycle was still there. Tommy turned another corner and continued to follow along the fields. He coasted down a long hill and stopped when he reached the bottom. He walked across the street, opposite the Flora Fields, and let his bike drop to the ground.

Tommy looked back again. The motorcycle had stayed at the top of the hill. It would serve as a beacon to Fisk, letting him know exactly where to go.

CHAPTER 17

Hidden Agenda

Safely inside the tree line, Tommy shifted into his cat form. His cat-eye view turned the blackness into a glowing green of branches and stones. He had forgotten to grab a flashlight, and he didn't want to take the risk of tripping. Feeling much more sure of himself, he pushed forward.

Tommy hoped he was able to get in and out of this situation without having to fight. Try as he might, he just couldn't picture a small gray kitty destroying the small army Fisk would almost definitely have along with him.

He found a babbling crick and followed it. The crickets and bullfrogs that had been so deafening a minute ago fell silent, like they were holding their breath.

If the directions he had been given were right, he was almost there. He could feel his hands shaking slightly, but he wasn't scared. He was excited. This was his chance to make up for losing the piece in Florida. This was his chance to recover the one his father had died to find.

As he neared the edge of the trees, he slowed and softened his considerably light footsteps. A long, careful examination of the clearing on the other side spiked his heart rate.

Just because I don't see anyone doesn't mean they aren't there, he reminded himself.

Tommy was certain the man on the motorcycle would have pointed Fisk and his men in this direction. However, he hadn't seen or heard anyone following him. As far as he could tell, he was alone.

He transformed back into his human shape, thinking it would be best to keep his small cat size a secret for as long as possible. He stepped past the trees and out into a grassy clearing.

Tommy walked to the crick and bent down. He put his hand in the cool water. It was a nice contrast against the humid night. A branch snapped behind him, but Tommy continued to kneel. When he stood back up, he turned, smiling.

The smile was returned by Marcellus Fisk.

As Tommy predicted, Fisk was surrounded by at least a dozen large, frightening men. A couple more slunk noiselessly out of the forest, bringing their number to fifteen.

Tommy and Fisk looked at each other, both acting as if they expected the other to speak first. Finally, Fisk gave in.

"What can I say, Tommy?" he asked. "You couldn't have asked for a nicer night to die. But, this must be strange for you. Knowing your father had taken his last steps over this same patch of grass. Knowing that he had stumbled and bled in the same spot you're standing now. And that, like you, he was no match for Badru."

Tommy's jaw clenched, but Asim had taught him not to show emotion to an enemy. Fisk's words hurt, but he couldn't let him know that.

"My father wasn't the only one hurt that night," Tommy said evenly. "And I believe it was my father who left with the statue."

"Left?" Fisk laughed, his voice echoing harshly on the trees. "You consider crawling away like a coward and dying in the street *leaving*? Then yes, I guess Husani *left* that night. But Badru's growing stronger by the minute. He's confident that I'm moments away from rebuilding our empire."

"Your empire? You expect me to believe Badru has promised to share his power with you?" Tommy asked.

Fisk's eyes snapped back to Tommy. He gave a quick, nervous laugh, and stepped forward.

"And why wouldn't he? Why wouldn't Badru reward his most loyal servant? For years I've searched for the remaining fragments of Ra's statue. I have sacrificed everything to make way for his rebirth. No one has given more than I have! His power will be my power!"

The space between Tommy and Fisk grew smaller with each step Fisk took. His eyes grew more crazed with each word. Tommy stood his ground, but his heart was pounding. More than ever he wished he had his necklace.

Fisk's hair looped wildly from his head and covered half his face. He turned his back to Tommy and pointed to the statue-still men standing behind him.

"Look at these faces, Bomani. These are the faces of men history will remember as heroes. The men who fought bravely for their leader in a time of great struggle. They will be remembered forever as the men who finally halted the cursed menace of the Bomani bloodline!"

"I'm sorry Fisk, but that isn't going to happen. Not tonight," Tommy said. He crossed his arms and tried to look confident.

"No?" Fisk turned back to Tommy and laughed until he ran out of breath. He put his hands to his ribs, as if he had laughed to the point of pain.

"The Bomani arrogance never ceases to amuse me. You are as much an idiot child as your father was an idiot man. Both of you believing you can win when there is nothing before you but defeat. Have you completely forgotten what happened the last time?"

Fisk unbuttoned his dark suit coat and blindly tossed it to a man behind him, who caught it. He marched slowly forward, stopping inches from Tommy. He bent down until they were face-to-face.

"I shot your friend and let him fall into a pool of alligators. I burned your girlfriend's house to the ground. I've had men following you for days, and you've had no idea. And tonight, I tricked you into leading me straight to the statue. You abandoned your friends to try to stop me, but instead you led me exactly where I wanted to be.

"You cannot stop me, Tommy Bomani. You cannot stop Badru. Badru's time has come again. There is nothing you can do about it."

Fisk reached out both hands and gripped Tommy powerfully by his shoulders. Fisk's eyes burned like a mad fire through the darkness, and his breath smelled foul. "Now, Tommy. Show me where your father hid the statue before I lose my temper."

Tommy gritted his teeth, disgusted by the touch of such a despicable person. His pulse fluttered and pounded, so he took a deep breath to calm it. When he was ready, he said, "Sorry Fisk. Can't do that."

Fisk snarled. "Then things are about to get a little painful for you."

Tommy shook his head. "It won't do any good. It was my turn to trick you."

Fisk paused.

Tommy winked. "The statue isn't here. I would never abandon my friends. You underestimated me."

CHAPTER 18

Wishing Well

Burt, Lily, and a black dog ran up to the old farm well. The dog made it first, and quickly shifted into her human form. Annie stared down into the well, then turned back to the other two.

"Burt, can I see the flashlight?" she asked.

Burt handed it to her from the ground, trying his best to force air back into his exhausted lungs. He rolled over onto his back and hit the light on his watch.

"It took us . . . ," Burt took a couple more deep breaths, and then tried talking again. " . . . ten minutes."

"Do you think that was fast enough?" Lily asked.

Annie pointed the flashlight in random directions around them. "If Fisk followed Tommy, and the statue piece really is in this well, then I hope so. But if either of those don't happen . . ."

"I guess it doesn't really matter, huh?" Lily finished. She followed the flashlight beam with her eyes, taking in the farmland surrounding them.

The area immediately around the well held only flowers and grass, but every other direction showed late-spring crops bursting through the ground.

Lily stuck a fingernail in her mouth and began chewing. "Oh man, I hope I was right. I would just die if the piece isn't in there."

"There's only one way to find out." Annie turned the flashlight onto Burt. "Still got the rope, Burt?"

Burt stood up and pulled a coiled brown rope from around his shoulder. He handed it to Annie. "I don't think I'm going to be able to fit in there, girls."

Annie shook her head. "Even if you could, there's no way we'd be able to lift you back out. It even looks too narrow for me to fit. It's going to have to be Lily."

Lily's eyes went wide and she put her hand to her mouth. "Me? I mean, I want to help but—"

"There's no time to argue." Annie began tying the rope around Lily's waist. "I know climbing into a dark well isn't exactly the help you thought you would give, but we need you."

Lily looked to Burt, who said, "Annie's right, Lily. You can do this. You already helped us figure out where the statue piece is. Now we just need you to get it out and bring it home."

Lily chewed more furiously on her nails. She paced away, but Annie yanked her back and continued working on her knots.

"You promise you'll pull me out?"

Burt smiled and put his hand gently on her shoulder. "No matter what."

Lily nodded. "Then I'll go."

"Great." Annie put one last cinch in the rope and pointed to the well. "Let's get moving. I don't know how much time we have, but it can't be a lot. The last thing we need is for Fisk's men to catch up to us."

Lily walked to the well and looked down. Annie handed her the flashlight, and Burt walked up beside her, the rest of the rope in his hands.

"If you run into any kind of trouble, just yell. I'll pull you right back up, okay?" he said.

Lily nodded and climbed onto the well's low stone edge. She peered down into the darkness and flicked on the flashlight.

"Lily?" Burt said. She turned and looked into his eyes. Hers were full of fear. His were full of pride. "I know you can do it. Good luck."

"Thanks," she said, and gently slid over the edge. Burt carefully let the rope drop, feeding it hand-over-hand into the well. Annie stood behind him, holding the rope with her strongest grip.

Burt peeked over the edge and saw the bouncing beam of the flashlight already a good distance down. "How is it down there?" he called.

Lily's voiced echoed back up. "It's cold. And it smells. I'd rather not talk about it, okay? There's a pretty good chance if I do I'm gonna ralph."

Burt laughed. "Sounds good. Just give a yell if you need anything."

Burt's giant hands passed the rope forward until it finally went slack. Lily must have reached the bottom. Annie and Burt walked up to the well and looked down. They held their breath and watched as the flashlight beam disappeared. A surprised gasp escaped Annie's throat.

"Where did the light go? Lily!"

There was no response. Burt grabbed the rope, then set it back down. Lily hadn't yelled to be taken back up, like they had planned. Annie stopped moving and just looked at him. They were both frozen with fright.

"Annie! Burt! Pull me up! Now!" Lily's high-pitched voice burst out of the well.

Burt jumped to the rope and Annie ran behind him. Both began pulling as fast and hard as they could. Burt's hands began to blister and burn, but he ignored the pain.

Finally Lily's head peeked above the edge. Burt grabbed her by the armpits and pulled her out in one swift move. They stumbled back and landed on the ground.

Lily laid on her side, curled into a ball and breathing deeply. She was caked with mud, dust, and spider webs. Her eyes opened and she smiled.

"I got it." Lily held out both hands. Wrapped tightly between them was the sixth shard of the Sun of Ra statue.

"You did it!" Annie yelled. "Thatta girl!"

Burt grabbed Lily in a hug. She giggled and kissed him quickly on the cheek. Burt set her down, his face red as fire.

"What do we do now?" Lily asked.

Annie picked up the flashlight and pointed it back to the woods. "We hightail it back to the warehouse and hope Tommy pulls off his end of the plan."

CHAPTER 19

Moment of Truth

isk's face shrunk in a fit of twitches and sharp breaths. His nostrils flared and his eyes nearly popped from his head. He pushed his fists to his temples. For a moment, Tommy thought he was angry enough to try crushing his own head.

Tommy took a wary step backward.

"What do you mean the piece isn't here?!" Fisk screamed.

"There isn't much more to it than that. It isn't here."

"Don't give me your lip, boy! Where is it?"

"You wouldn't be able to find where my father hid it even if I told you, Fisk. Because it isn't there anymore," Tommy said.

"Does this seem like a game to you, Bomani?" Fisk bellowed. He stepped forward and punched Tommy in the stomach. Tommy crumpled to the ground, gasping for breath. "Do you think this is fun, playing with your life like this?"

Tommy tried to speak, but he couldn't. He felt like a bag of lead was pushing down on his lungs.

"So what did you do? You and your little friends must have figured out where the piece was." Fisk paced as he spoke, and spit flew from his lips. "And then you thought you'd come up with a plan and be the hero again. Well it isn't going to happen like that this time."

Fisk bent over Tommy. He lowered his voice into a harsh scraping noise. "Your friends may have found the piece, but they've lost you. This is the last time you'll cross me, Bomani. Don't think I haven't noticed that you aren't wearing your necklace. Without that extra power, you're defenseless. Tonight Badru will finally be rid of the Bomani plague."

Tommy looked his enemy straight in the eyes, and pushed all the air out of his lungs with one huge bellow.

"Now!" he screamed. *"Do it now!"*

Powerful spotlights burst from four hidden corners, blinding everyone in the grassy opening. Police officers in dark clothing spilled out from within the caves, from behind the trees, and from every other imaginable hiding place. They tackled every man they saw. In under a minute Fisk and all of his men were on their stomachs with their hands cuffed behind their backs.

Tommy stood over Fisk. Next to him stood Detective Matthews.

"Burt finally got ahold of you," Tommy stated.

"Just in the nick of time, from the looks of it," the detective answered.

A police officer walked up to Detective Matthews. "We got 'em all, Detective. A couple almost made it back into the forest, but we stopped 'em before they got too far."

"Excellent work, Sergeant. Start loading them into the trucks, and we'll get back to the station."

The officer walked away to relay his orders to the others. Tommy looked at Detective Matthews and motioned to Fisk. "Are you sure your guys will be able to keep him locked up this time?"

Detective Matthews nodded confidently. "Last time no one knew who he was. Now that I'm in town, I'll personally make sure he's given extra attention."

The detective smiled, and then looked at Tommy strangely. "Tommy, it sounded like you had already left by the time Burt got me on the phone. What would you have done if we hadn't been able to be here?"

"He would have died," Fisk said from the ground.

Tommy shook his head. "I don't know. I guess it's a good thing you came."

Suddenly the spotlights went dark. Everyone froze, unsure what had happened. Detective Matthews pulled the gun from his hip and yelled, "Johnson! Who killed the lights?"

"Wasn't us, Detective," came the response.

Detective Matthews put his hand on Tommy's chest. "Why don't you get behind me, son. I'm not quite sure what—"

A gush of fiery light leapt up from the center of crick and draped the area with a blaze ten times as strong as the spotlights.

In the middle of the light's origin, hovering over the water, was a dark man in a dark, worn cloak. His face wore jagged scars thousands of years old.

Badru had arrived.

CHAPTER 20

Badru Rising

'Fisk!" Badru's voice came out howling and hollow, an ancient wind bouncing across the desert. "You have failed me!"

Fisk stared up at the glowing figure and broke into a fit of laughter. "But here is the boy! Bomani is yours!"

Six gunshots rang out next to Tommy, and he dropped to the ground in surprise. Detective Matthews watched in dismay as his bullets flew straight through their target and into the hillside behind it. He lowered his weapon in awe.

"A cowardly attempt," Badru hissed. "Luckily for you what you see is not my true form, or your life would be snuffed without hesitation." He pointed to Fisk. "As would yours, weakling. But for now I have only a message."

Tommy stood and faced the incredible specter. He couldn't believe this was happening. It was like something out of a dream.

"What do you want, Badru?" Tommy asked.

"Don't you speak my name as if we are equals! I am royalty! You are the remains of a disgusting bloodline unworthy of the godly blood it carries. My prophecy declares that we will fight, and you will die. It is time for us to meet and to begin the end."

Tommy clenched his fists and yelled back, "Too bad I think your prophecy is a bunch of garbage."

Badru laughed a slow, arrogant laugh, and Tommy felt his blood run cold. "It matters not what you think, child. The future has been foretold. One unclaimed piece of Ra's statue remains, in my land of kings. You will attempt to claim it. You will be denied, and I will finally rule as the most powerful pharaoh the world has known. Come to me, boy, and come to your glorious death."

Badru's light vanished, and they were again draped in darkness.

Within seconds the floodlights powered back to life, revealing a lazy-flowing crick and nothing else. Tommy stared at the spot Badru had been without moving. His fists were still clenched at his side. He turned to Detective Matthews.

"Can you give me a ride?" he asked. "I need to speak with Asim. Now."

CHAPTER 21

A Victory Short-lived

Tommy ran as fast as he could into the warehouse, and Detective Matthews trailed behind him. They had found nothing but an empty bed at the hospital. No one on the staff knew where Asim had gone.

The first one to see Tommy was Annie. She met him a few steps from the door and wrapped him in a hug.

"Hey, Cuz, you made it! Did the plan work? Did you get Fisk?" she asked.

Tommy's face didn't return the delighted expression Annie was showing. "Yeah, we got him. You guys find the statue piece?"

Burt and Lily ran out of the back office. "You're darn right we did!" Burt yelled. "Lily was right. It was at the bottom of the well. There was a little room off to the side, and it was just sitting there, waiting for us!"

Tommy breathed a quick sigh of relief but kept pushing forward. "Good. Excellent job."

Detective Matthews had caught up. "Is Asim here? He wasn't at the hospital."

Burt pointed to the office he had just come out of. "Yeah, he's—"

"I'm right here." Asim stepped out of the office with a large smile on his face.

Tommy and Detective Matthews both stopped and let out the breath they had each been holding.

The detective spoke first. "Thank goodness, Asim. When you weren't at the hospital, we'd worried—"

"What, that Fisk had gotten to me?" he interrupted, smiling. He looked more healthy than Tommy had ever seen him, and more happy.

"No. That Badru had," Tommy stated flatly.

Asim's face twittered with confusion. "Badru? What do you mean?"

"He appeared after we arrested Fisk," Detective Matthews said.

"What do you mean, *he appeared?*" Asim asked.

Annie, Lily, and Burt crowded around. The joyous expressions they had been wearing were gone.

Tommy spoke, "It wasn't really him. It was some kind of holograph or something."

"More likely it was telepathic display. He projected an image of himself with his mind. Another one of his more frightening abilities," Asim said. "What did he tell you?"

"He talked about the last missing piece," Tommy said. "He said that I have to go claim it, and that he has to stop me. He talked about the prophecy."

Asim looked to the ground and nodded. Then, he looked back up and into Tommy's eyes.

"Badru is wrong, but he is also right," Asim said.

They waited for him to continue.

"He is wrong in his absolute faith in his prophecy. What he has foretold is only one possibility. Do not confuse his certainty with a guaranteed outcome. If I thought differently, there is no way I would allow you to confront him."

"But you think I should."

Asim nodded. He added, "That is where he is right. The time has come to claim the rest of the statue. You can only do that through defeating Badru. He has already regained the power to project himself halfway across the globe. If we wait much longer, who knows how much stronger he will become."

Tommy looked to Burt, Annie, and Lily.

"What do you want us to do?" Tommy asked Asim.

"For now, we must tell your parents that you have all returned safely. They are worried, and we must calm their minds."

Asim and Detective Matthews walked to the office, then turned back around before entering. "But while you are with your families, you must also collect your passports and pack. You can take only one bag apiece. Detective Matthews and I will make arrangements, and we will all meet back here in ten hours. In the morning, we leave for Egypt."

Burt, Annie, and Lily hesitated, and then began to walk for the door. Tommy stayed put.

"Wait," Tommy said. They did as he said and looked back to him. Asim and Detective Matthews did the same, but Tommy looked to his friends.

"I need you guys to know something," he continued. "Without your help, I wouldn't have stood a chance against Fisk. I know that for a fact.

You have made the difference every time. That said, I want to offer you three the chance to stay here."

"What are you talking about, Tom?" Burt asked.

Asim slipped the statue piece from around his neck and handed it to Tommy. Tommy took it by the chain and stared at it thoughtfully.

"We're not just dealing with Fisk anymore. If what Asim has told me is true, Badru is a hundred times more dangerous. Especially if he's as strong as he seemed tonight. Just putting him in jail isn't going to be an option. We're going to have to kill him. If you aren't comfortable with that . . . I want you to know that I appreciate everything you've done. I respect your decision if you don't want to come."

"Tommy, I—," Burt started, but couldn't finish. He looked to the ground. Lily hugged his arm and dropped her eyes to the same spot.

Tommy bit his lip nervously.

"Bomani, that's gotta be the stupidest thing you've ever said." Annie smirked.

Burt and Lily looked up.

"Do you honestly think we'd put in this much effort just to watch you finish things up and take all the credit?" Annie said. "You're darn right we're coming. And we're not coming back here until that mummified freak is as dead as he should have been two thousand years ago. Right, guys?"

Burt and Lily looked each other in the eye, and then looked to Annie.

"Absolutely," Lily said.

"Can't imagine you leaving without us, Tommy. It just wouldn't be right," Burt said.

Annie nodded. "You can't get rid of us, Tommy. We're a team. We're doing this together, or not at all."

Tommy stood still. He looked over to his friends, and then to Asim. He pulled the necklace over his head until it rested comfortably against his chest.

"In that case, you'd better grab those other statue pieces before we leave, Asim. I'm thinking we're going to need all the firepower we can get."

Tommy smiled and ran past his friends toward the door. He turned around and waved them forward. "What are you waiting for? Pack your bags and tell your families you love them. We've got a battle to fight."

CONTINUE THE ADVENTURE WITH

Tommy Bomani: Teen Warrior

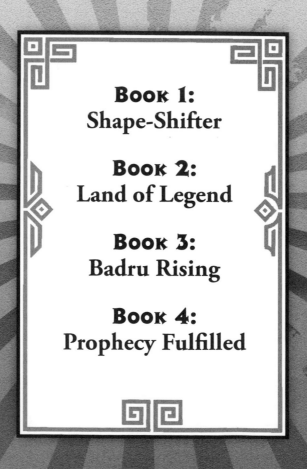

Book 1:
Shape-Shifter

Book 2:
Land of Legend

Book 3:
Badru Rising

Book 4:
Prophecy Fulfilled